Snowball Fight!

by **Jimmy Fallon**

illustrated by **Adam Stower**

SCHOLASTIC INC.

New York Toronto London Auckland Sydney
Mexico City New Delhi Hong Kong Buenos Aires

ISBN-13: 978-0-439-93067-3
ISBN-10: 0-439-93067-7

12 11 10 9 8 7 6 5 4 3 2   7 8 9 10 11 12/0

Printed in the U.S.A.   40

First Scholastic printing, January 2007

Designed by Edie Weinberg

To my elementary school in Saugerties, NY—St. Mary
of the Snow—for giving me and my sister plenty
of snow days to play together

J.F.

For Nan, with love

A.S.

Snow day! School's closed!

Snow is white. Half my height!

Somewhere, out there, snowball fight!

Snowball,
snowball,
snowball fight!

Long johns.

Moon boots.

Woolly hats

and hand-me-down snowsuit.

No time for breakfast,
already late.

Pretend I don't hear when Mom yells,

"Wait!"

Fort is ready.

Munitions stored.

Way too quiet.
Getting bored.

Spied around but didn't see...

fifteen snowballs coming at me.

ATTACK!

Snowball, snowball, snowball fight!

Snowball, snowball, snowball fight!

Out of ammo,
trapped in fort.
Enemy approaching,
need support.

Sneak attack. Plan revealed.

Use your toboggan as a shield.

Snowball, snowball, snowball fight!

Snowball, snowball, snowball fight!

**Run back home,
in retreat.**

Snow down my back, soaking-wet feet.

Pj's, cocoa, fireside truce.

One last snowball, future use.